The ARAL MILL MURDERS

A Novella
By
Richard Trevae

Silas — Enjoy!

The ARAL MILL MURDERS / Richard Trevae
ISBN-13: 978-0615627625
ISBN-10: 0615627625
First Edition EBook: May 2012
Editor: Richard Trevae
Printed in the United States of America

Other books /short stories by Richard Trevae:

The Dalton Crusoe Series

The TARASOV SOLUTION
The ISRAELI BETRAYAL
The SECRET TEMPLAR ALLIANCE

Short Stories

The Last Season
Rhythms of Leelanau

Readers may contact the author at: www.richardtrevae.com
and richard@trevae.com

Published by Treline Publishing,
a unit of Treline Development Group, Inc.
1675 E. Mt. Garfield Road
Norton Shores, MI 49444

Printed in the U.S.A.

10 9 8 7 6 5 4 3 2 1

Author Notes

I have been having fun creating fiction from *reality-inspired-events* resulting in three novels comprising the Dalton Crusoe sagas. As a fiction author one can be drawn to a piece of history but not be restrained by the *historical facts* when conceiving a plausible new story. To take a piece of history, preferably engaging history, and twist it into a credible take-off on reality is what many authors of suspense and thriller novels seek.

Similarly an author can be drawn to write about his own experiences and feelings yet in a fictionalized setting. That is what I did in short stories, The Last Season, and again in Rhythms of Leelanau, each inspired by the beauty of Leelanau County Michigan, along Lake Michigan's sand-dune bounded shore. In a new twist, I studied the data involving three historical events...the sinking of the Westmoreland, chronicled by Ross Richardson, the twin murders committed by Charles T. Wright in 1889, and his inexplicable release from life in prison, eleven years later.

I hope you enjoy the novella.

Acknowledgements

To my wife Vicki, who always has supported and critiqued my writing, along with being my first reader, and to Linda Freeman, our travel concierge, who has provided a bounty of locales, photos, advice, and background history to keep this author well supplied with material.

This novella would not be complete without an acknowledgement to Dave Taghon, the "Empire Historian", who first turned me onto the historical events which led to the creation of this historical fiction novella...The ARAL MILL MURDERS.

Lastly, to my children JoAnn, along with her husband Kraig, and John, and my extended family, who have followed and encouraged my musings.

DEDICATION

Jacqueline, Tyler and Megan

CAST OF CHARACTERS

Charles T. Wright, "Charley", Aral Mill Owner and Manager

Sara Wright, Charley's wife

Fred Cossett, Sara's brother and company store manager

James Wright, Charley's brother

Joseph Wright, Uncle to Charles and James

Dr. Frank Thurber, Aral Physician and Lake County Treasurer

Deputy Neil Marshall, Benzonia Sheriff Deputy

Sheriff A.B. Case, Benzonia Sheriff

Attorney Covell, Benzonia Prosecuting Attorney

Lahala, Aral Mill foreman, Ottawa Indian

Governor Hazen S. Pingree, Michigan Governor 1897-1901

Prelude

Near Sleeping Bear Point, Lake Michigan, December 8, 1854

The captain should have never left the Wisconsin shore and struck out for the Manitous with the storm warnings. The December wind continued to strengthen as the big ship, Westmoreland, crashed and rolled against the sea-sized waves. Winter storms were known to rise quickly on Lake Michigan and stir up the big lake as if it were a "sea". The storm attacking the Westmoreland now was testing its durability. Joseph Wright's thoughts about the ship's sea-worthiness took over his mind as he looked out from the bridge at the ice covered deck, fearing the worst. As a precautionary move, Wright put on his heavy canvas caped storm coat, stuffed his hands in the large pockets for warmth and studied the captain.

"How are the pumps holding up in the engine room Joe?" Captain Clark checked his watch — 4:00 a.m. six hours after the snow and ice storm hit with gale-force winds.

"If our leakage gets no worse, and we can get to a protected harbor soon, we should be able to repair the hull and remove the water." Joseph Wright, the Westmoreland's first engineer, had two hand pumps running along with the bilge pump, yet the water continued to flood the engine room. He hoped, and prayed, that the captain's fears, a serious hull breach, due to the massive ice buildup could be avoided. The wood burning steamer had to get to the protective harbor at South Manitou.

"I'll go back down to the engine room and check on things." Captain Clark nodded his agreement to his first engineer. Clark held his eyes focused on the icy deck lit only by the bridge lights reflecting on the dense horizontal snow racing across the bow.

Wright shot down the narrow staircase to the engine room. The ship was being thrown side-to-side, crashing downward as the bow attempted to cut through the eighteen-foot waves. The water leaking through the stressed hull timbers sloshed about and hissed into steam as it splashed against the hot cast iron boiler. He watched deckhand Hannegan stoking wood into the burner chamber and asked, "Is the water rising still?"

"Aye, I put a mark on that column an hour ago near the wood storage; it's now covered by four inches." Hannegan pointed to the column. Wright moved to the column and studied the rugged, wooded post.

"No. It's now six inches above your mark. The hull is opening up with the heaving and the ice buildup. We could break apart." Wright looked to Hannegan who stood in water just below his knees, shaking as much from fear as the cold. "Keep pumping, the captain is trying to reach South Manitou." Hannegan returned to his hand pump whispering an Irish prayer.

The storm grew stronger while the ship's hull weakened more and more, flooding the engine room to the point where the boiler fires could not be maintained. By 8 a.m. the Manitous were visible and the ship was adrift without power. The deck disappeared under three feet of ice. The storm's fury maintained a relentless assault on the ship and crew for over sixteen hours. The captain struggled to right the ship for hours and at 3 p.m. finally ordered the life boats and yawl be dispatched.

Wright studied the engine room one last time when he heard, "All hands and passengers get to the lifeboats, now!" It was Captain Clark yelling from the bridge.

The ship began sinking fast, listing hard from side-to-side, dumping cargo into the galley and engine room. Barrels of whiskey and flour floated about knocking crew and equipment to the hull as the ship rolled. Joseph Wright made sure his men were headed up on deck. Hannegan was still manning his hand pump—knee deep in the freezing water.

"Get outta here, you crazy Irishman, she's breakin' up...going down."

Hannegan stopped pumping, grabbed his oilskin coat and remarked, "I hate to give up sir...but I don't fancy going down with her. You comin'...?" The first engineer nodded and waved Hannegan up the staircase.

As Wright reached for the staircase hole a wave threw the boat hard to the starboard side and a whiskey barrel shattered to bits against his back. He went down toward the deck, semi-conscious, lungs filling with freezing water. Several moments later he seemed to be in a dreamlike state...seeing, yet not feeling anything. The last of the lingering engine fires spread yellow hues over the rising, turbulent water. The waves came cascading through the portside hull and created a slow moving moment of strange bright flashes, surrounding Wright as he sank deeper and deeper. Scores of small, brilliant bursts were everywhere as he drifted into a semi-conscious daze. Wright felt limp and bewildered as he watched the amazing image before him as barrel fragments dispersed; death was approaching. The scene went dark; he felt nothing until a tug, then voices, and finally the face of Hannegan yelling something.

"Mister Wright... Joe...wake up. I gotcha, now come on...we're agoing down, fast." Hannegan had come back down the engine ladder hole and grabbed Wright's jacket collar lifting him from the flooded engine room deck. He pulled him up above the waterline just as Joe realized he'd been saved by Hannegan. They ran stumbling across the rolling deck and fell into the waiting life boat, already filled with nine men. As they pulled on the oars to escape the Westmoreland, she broke at her main beam and headed down bow first. A line whipping in the fierce wind tangled with another one of the life boats trying to escape the Westmoreland's demise. A passenger in the life boat struggled to cut the tangled line before the small craft rolled over. In fifteen seconds the big ship disappeared, blowing open cabin quarters and storage rooms as the punishing waves smashed windows, doors and walls amid screams of those lost to the storm. The wash swirling at the surface tossed the tethered life boat on her side dumping all eight passengers into the freezing waters. Paul Pelkey, Wright, and two others, pulled hard on the long oars. Hannegan risked being thrown from the craft as he stood and tied off several lines snapping in the wind, securing the small sail to the mast. The heavy rolling waves thrust the bow upward only to let it crash into the trough of the next wave a few seconds later. Every advance to the eastern shoreline also found the yawl blown south by the ferocious northwest wind. Three hours later the wind relented a bit and the men got the yawl near the shore at Otter Creek. Pelkey jumped out into five feet of freezing water clutching a heavy rope to pull the craft to the beach when he went under water. Wright vaulted over the bow and pulled Pelkey up.

"Come on Paul...we're so close, let's get this boat to shore." Pelkey finally got his footing, stood and helped Wright on the rope. Hannegan joined them in the water and moments later the yawl was beached, tilted over on her starboard side as the remaining eight men jumped to shore. The snow and ice were a foot deep with the temperature hovering around 20 degrees.

"Anyone have dry matches?" Pelkey was shivering uncontrollably as was Wright.

"Aye, I've got some in a tin, in my pocket...I pray they're dry." Hannegan shook as his hand ventured into his oilskin coat vest packet. All eyes remained glued on the Irishman as he withdrew the small tin. Hannegan's hand was wet, dripping with water. All eleven, dripping wet men released a desperate collective sigh; the tin was drenched. Hannegan smiled as he opened the tin and revealed ten, long, wooden-stick matches, each with its end covered in candle wax. The group looked on curiously.

"A trick me pa taught me as I went to sea." The Irish deckhand took a stick, scraped off the candle wax revealing a fresh, dry match head.

Pelkey barked out, "We must get some wood and pine branches." Six men ran towards the woods and cleared a protected spot a hundred yards from the shore and formed a brush pile stacked to protect the green pine boughs tucked beneath. The first match Hannegan struck flared immediately and began a smoldering fire. Minutes later a large, blazing fire warmed the freezing survivors. The mood grew quiet, as the flames warmed and dried the men. All considered their status against the backdrop of seventeen lost souls. After ten minutes of huddling close to the roaring fire, Joseph Wright sat nearby on a log. His pants, shirt, and wool sweater appeared to be on fire as the water vapor re-condensed after leaving his heated garments. He began sketching a map detailing the events of the last hours. Paul Pelkey took note and asked, "What are you doing Joe?"

"Something happened to me as she broke up...something very confusing. It's hard to explain. But I want to document exactly where we went down, the weather conditions, and look for the wreck next summer." Wright's expression was strange; Pelkey sensed the first engineer came very close to death on the Westmoreland.

"Really? What could make you want to come back? We damn near died."

Joseph Wright stopped his scribbling, looked out to the lake, reached in his jacket pocket and retrieved something,... holding it out for Pelkey to examine.

Pelkey stared into Wright's hand finding it difficult to speak. Several seconds of silence confirmed both men were mesmerized. Then Pelkey managed to compose himself and remarked, "Let me help with that map. I'll come back with you next summer."

* * *

Racine Wisconsin, April 1881

Joseph Wright lived the bulk of his life on the water, first as a sailor and then an engineer aboard the Great Lakes steamers. His last commission as first engineer aboard the Westmoreland, a mighty ship designed to handle the rough weather occasioning the Great Lakes in winter, lingered vividly in his mind. At one-hundred-sixty feet long and displacing 665 tons she was an impressive craft. Wright felt privileged to have worked her despite that when she sank in December 1854 off the Manitou Islands he nearly died along with seventeen others who perished. Now nearing death, Wright felt compelled to relay his experience to nephews Charles and James, his only living relation. He laid restless, breathing labored and appearing very pale. A stroke, months earlier, had left him limited use of his legs and left arm. He noticed the two young men approach and sit next to his hospital bed.

"Uncle Joe, it's me, James, and Charles. Do you remember us?"

Wright focused his eyes on the rugged looking men and smiled. "Hey boys, it's so good to see you. Thanks for coming to see me. How is the lumber business going for you?" Wright held out his right hand and grabbed Charles arm pulling him closer.

"My brother would be so proud of how well you two have done running the lumber mill after he died." Charles and James smiled at their father's older brother and could see he was weak and frail. "Help me sit up in bed; I have something to tell you both." Charles lifted the old man up and James pressed a pillow behind his uncle's back. Joseph Wright appeared very different than the man his nephews remembered from their youth. In his younger days Joseph Wright was an adventurer, story-teller and man-of-the-world. His time at sea took him along the east coast ports on merchant ships and eventually down the St. Lawrence Seaway serving the Canadian ports and the major cities of the Great Lakes. When the steamers crowded out the clipper ships, Joseph used his considerable mechanical skills to secure an engineer position on lumber and coal transports. It was twenty-eight years ago when he landed a cushy job on a line of smaller passenger tourist boats designed to travel the Great Lakes and deliver tourists and dry goods to the small ports along Michigan's western shore. It was his second season on the Westmoreland when she broke up in a powerful early winter storm and went down near Sleeping Bear Point.

Charles and James pulled their chairs tight to their uncle's bed waiting for him to speak. Once the floor nurse left the room and closed the door he began. "Do you remember when I worked the Westmoreland boys?"

"Sure, we remember. We were about ten or eleven years old. It went down and you and others had to paddle to shore in freezing weather, right?" James looked to the older-by-a-year Charles for confirmation.

"Right! It sank off Michigan's west coast in December." Charles remembered the event.

"Yes, that's the way it happened. It was winter and I damn near died from the cold and snow. It took me six months to recover and then make my way back to the area in the summer." The brothers, now in their late thirties, remembered the tragedy that nearly took their uncle Joe.

"I always hoped your dad and I could have finished what I am about to tell you, but he died way too young and you boys were busy caring for and running his lumber business. So, I tried to finish the job alone. I'm sorry; I failed at that...now it's your chance to pick up where I left off...years ago."

Joseph Wright paid the price with his health for decades of smoking and drinking while ignoring warning symptoms. His weakened heart practically invalided him ten years earlier, just about the time his lungs showed blood when he coughed. Now at sixty-six years old his prognosis was terminal.

"What is it you failed to finish, Joe?" Charles and James feared their uncle was losing his mind and had fantasized another adventure from his youth. Nevertheless, they waited respectfully for their uncle to resume his story.

"Just as the Westmoreland fired her boilers to depart from Racine, back in December 1854, a covered wagon pulled by four chestnut Morgans stopped at our dock. Two men pulled canvas back and unloaded thirty barrels of whiskey and then covered them again with the canvas down in our hold. Another man on horseback stood watch armed with a 40-caliber James Warner revolving rifle. It was a strange scene...the way it happened."

Charles smirked and said, "Nice cargo. It must have made the crew happy to see all that booze...maybe sample it a bit." James cracked a smile as well and looked for a reaction from Joseph.

"The ship was minutes from departing dock and all hands were busy tending to lines and the passengers. I was the only one to physically see the barrels go into the hold. I signed for the cargo just as we tied off the Racine dock. Neither Captain Clark or first mate, Paul Pelkey saw the cargo board."

Suddenly Joseph clutched his mouth and coughed violently, blood spraying the bed sheets. Charles jumped and reached for a towel, wetted it, and threw it to James who wiped his uncle's face and mouth. The frail man gasped for breath and pointed to a small dresser opposite his bed.

"What is it Uncle Joe? Something you need? Shall I get a nurse?"

"No!" Joseph again pointed to the dresser...struggling to breathe.

Charles moved to the small cabinet pulling open the top drawer. "It... it's in here?"

"Brown packet with a string strap...bring it here." The frail, old sailor was still gasping for air. "Open it, there's a map I sketched with Pelkey twenty-seven years ago."

Charles withdrew a folded piece of heavy brown wrapping paper approximately eighteen inches by three feet. The paper folds were worn and tattered having been opened and folded many times over the years. Charles brought it over to James and laid it on the bed before their uncle.

"That's where the Westmoreland went down." Joseph moved his shaky hand and pointed to a spot near the Sleeping

Bear Point south of the Manitous. The map contained incredible detail and an "X" identifying the location where the ship broke up and went down. Dashed lines seemed to track the life boat's hapless route to the mainland. Notes and markings described the hike they took to find shelter. Near the upper left corner a few sentences described the final hours before the big ship sank. A dated, daily log describing the conditions once the men arrived on shore followed: wind speed and direction, snowfall amounts, sky conditions, and temperatures filled the left side of the paper. The names Paul Pelkey and Joseph Wright were penned in the lower right hand corner of the map. As the brothers studied the old map, then looking to their uncle as he continued his tale.

"It's still there...go find it. Pelkey and I tried in 1874...found the wreck and meant to salvage." The coughing erupted again, blood spewing out Joseph's mouth and nose. He wrenched in pain. Charles tried to steady his uncle who slouched in pain in the bed.

"I'm getting a doctor!" James ran to the door.

"No! No!...listen to me. Find it boys...no one knows of this except now you. Paul Pelkey died in 1876. I'm the only one left."

The coughing began again, more violently now. James opened the door to the hallway and called for help. Moments later two doctors and a nurse arrived and hovered over Joseph Wright. The frail old sailor never coughed again, despite frantic actions by the medical team to force air into Joseph's lungs with a hand held squeezable bag and face mask. Minutes passed, steady activity seemed to smother Joseph. Ten minutes later one of the doctors came over to Charles and James, who were ordered to move away while they worked on their patient, and spoke. "I'm sorry he was just too weak for us to save him. He has passed on...his heart simply gave out. I'll leave you two alone a moment."

Charles and James were speechless, looked at each other and then the map still clutched in Charles' hand. James looked back at his uncle and said, "I have no idea what he and dad were expecting to find...the ship, whiskey barrels, flour barrels or the ship's log."

“Yeah, I’m baffled. He certainly wanted to explain this map.” Charles rubbed his neck and then remarked, “Well, I guess we now have another reason for me to take that mill job in Aral.”

Both men thought back to a discussion not two days earlier. At that time, Charles Wright pondered taking a job offer to manage the Aral mill. He and James decided then it was a great first step to expand their lumber business and eventually combine the Racine and Aral operations.

“Right. Aral is very close to the spot Uncle Joe marked where the Westmoreland went down. Maybe I can find some very aged whiskey in barrels.” Neither brother found the flip remark comforting.

James looked into Charles’ sad face and said, “I gonna miss the old guy.”

Charles wiped his moist eyes and added, “Let’s get a drink to remember him.”

CHAPTER--ONE

Northwest Lower Michigan, August 1889

I knew nothing of Charles T. Wright before 1883 when he noticed my sister, Sara Cossett, and began to romance her. I had my doubts then and in time my worst fears were confirmed. For reasons I did not understand Sara was smitten with this lumberman brut of intemperate disposition and debauchery. Even his brother, James, back in Racine Wisconsin openly spoke ill of his nature and propensity to drunkenness and fighting. Nevertheless, my sister fell in love with the big talker and loud mouth mill manager in Aral, Michigan. Wright knew how to be charming, and used his considerable verbal skills and persuasive personality to get his way. When that approach failed, fighting was his last resort. Sara saw all this and still married the man in 1884 despite my concerns, which in truth I kept mainly to myself.

At first, when Wright began to manage the white pine lumber mill in 1881for owner Dr. Arthur O'Leary, a landowner and lumber speculator, things went well. Wright, or Charley to his friends, was best described as a good "company man" back then.

In the fall of 1883 I took a job managing the company books for Dr. O'Leary, and moved to Aral, along with my younger sister Sara. Wright even impressed me, C.F. (Fred) Cossett, when he soon asked me to become manager of the company store newly built directly across Otter Creek from the mill. In fairness, Wright was a first-rate, strong manager; the mill grew as the forests downstate in Muskegon and Grand Haven were totally harvested. By 1886 Wright somehow manage to lease the entire operation from O'Leary and finance the mill expansion. In 1888, O'Leary sold the lease to a Helen Davis of Brookline, Massachusetts, yet Wright retained the lease and made the payments. I was allowed to keep the company store well provisioned and we made a good living. The forests around Otter Creek were mature and dense; and the lumber buyers were regularly frequenting Aral offering contracts for white pine lumber. Business was good, people settled in little Aral, and for the most part the community prospered. Yet Wright couldn't refrain from his bad habits. Many evenings after work he would appear drunk talking loudly in the streets, laughing one minute and ready to pick a fight the next. A scrapper, Wright could take a punch and deliver one as well. My sister simply ignored the bad behavior and always said he was a good husband with a caring heart. Despite the crazy behavior Wright commanded respect, and people genuinely liked him when he was sober and not begging for a fight. He seemed to behave best when he would take off a few hours alone and fish along the Lake Michigan shore at Otter Creek extending far out waist deep on a sand bar. I guess that's what kept Sara content...that and the occasional love song he would belt out with gusto after a few drinks.

With the steady success of the mill Wright grew more emboldened, adding crew to the mill operation and hiring scores of workers to harvest lumber all winter waiting for spring when the mill would again start up production. Almost every week lumber speculators would arrive in little Aral or nearby Frankfort to visit Wright and his mill operation. He was quite the salesman and could bargain hard without getting folks upset, usually getting his price and more. Everything about his persona signaled Wright was used to getting his way. His negotiating style was one in which he first made one feel important by sharing casual compliments, being respectful and convincingly interested in one's objectives, and then skillfully finding the words to get his counterpart to accept his terms. It was almost hypnotic when he made his "magic" work on hard-headed lumber speculators. Moreover, he bragged that he never missed a delivery schedule—which impressed lumber buyers— a fact that closed many deals. Charley Wright could talk his way through most challenges to him getting the order. People respected that part of his character; I know I did, and so did his mill workers.

Throughout all this his bad behavior continued to burst forth—actually getting worse as the mill expanded. Eventually Wright built a house in Aral, across the creek and east of the mill. He and Sara moved in and life looked wonderful from her perspective; home, money, travel and security. That's just about when it all began to tumble down.

CHAPTER--TWO

August 1889, Aral Michigan

I opened the company store at the same time I did every weekday at 7:30 a.m. As I swept off the front porch to the company store Charles Wright walked up. He carried a stringer of five nice sized fish. “Morning Fred. I’m expecting a few downstate lumber buyers this afternoon. Any rooms clean at the hotel if they stay the night?”

“Good morning Charley. You’re up a bit early aren’t you? Went fishing?” My tone of voice alerted my brother-in-law I was not pleased with him. His bad behavior the night before typically meant he’d sleep off his drunkenness till 9 a.m. or so.

“Yup. Got up about six and caught these beauties in about thirty minutes. Any rooms?”

“Yeah, should be a couple rooms at least. That family from Chicago took the Frankfort steamer from here to Glen

Haven last evening." I kept sweeping and noticed a blood smear. Charley took notice.

"I'm sorry Fred, but that fur-trapper guy was really getting under my skin...showing off like that."

I swept the bloody tooth into the street. "Maybe, but did you have to beat him till he blanked out? That nice Chicago family had planned to stay two more nights until they saw you in action damn near killing that old trapper."

"I didn't like the way he talked in front of my wife...damn showoff…and he weren't all that old. Besides, he told me to mind my own business when I asked him to quiet down. " Charley pulled his rumpled handkerchief from his back pocket and wiped his swollen mouth and split lip. I glanced at him and smirked at the way he always justified his foul behavior.

As I looked about the small town the only movement was the yard workers at the Aral mill. The morning crew started at 7 a.m. sharp and the mill foreman, Peter Lahala, an English speaking Ottawa Indian, was dependable, getting all forty workers moving. Six men oversaw the stacked logs near the roll-way feeding the floating stockpile of timber into Otter

Creek. They held snag-hooks for pulling logs unto the steam driven chain belt up to the mill's second level where the large ripping saw operated. As the logs moved up the ramp water fell off the bark and splashed over the belt sounding much like rainfall. The saw produced a steady high pitched screech, which then changed to a dull roar as the logs were pushed by hand into the spinning blade. Every fifteen seconds the saw repeated the noise cycle providing a pleasant rhythm with which Charley could gage the production rate. Both Charley and I noticed the familiar "mill music" announcing the morning start of production.

"I feel it's gonna be a peach of a day Fred. I'll be over for lunch with the lumber buyers." Charley offered his standard broad smile and optimistic view of life as he handed me the stringer for storing the fish under sawdust and ice. He nodded, turned and headed toward the mill.

I waved a goodbye and returned to my porch sweeping, when I noticed Sara, my sister, peering out her upstairs bedroom window at her husband as he strolled to the mill.

* * *

The mill was the literal life blood for the small town of Aral. During the winter the woods were full of lumberjacks, mostly Europeans and native Indians, set up in canvas tent camps for up to 140 men. They harvested the prime pine timber and hauled it by horse drawn carts to the staging areas near Otter Creek. As winter gave way to spring, the mill resumed operations processing the logs into planks, beams, and dimensioned lumber for construction. Once the ports along Lake Michigan opened up, the lumber buyers traveled north to the mills along the shoreline and made purchase commitments. The spring and early summer had been good for the mill now filling one or two lumber barges each week. As August approached, the mill work force peaked at forty-five men handling the sawing operation, maintenance, and loading functions.

As Charles T. Wright reached the mill entrance Lahala approached his boss. “You bring buyers through mill today, boss?”

“Yes, that’s right. I’ll meet them at the hotel and then bring them over. Afterwards I’ll take them over to the company store for a lunch. Make sure the ripping saw is running and the dogs are set for a run of 2-by-12 rough sawn planks...that's what they need."

"I'll have it all runnin' boss...and I'll clean up the bark piles soose they can move around."

"Right! That's what I wanna see Lahala."

Lahala made his mark early on at the Aral Mill, frequently functioning as an interpreter between the Ottawa Indians' speech and the sloppy English attempted by the Finlanders, Swedes, and Polish immigrants working at the mill. He was smart, hard-working, respected and capable of leading the workforce in a manner that pleased Wright. The Europeans held the few technical positions including the job of carriage operator who also adjusted the setworks and dogs to the desired thickness. Yet Lahala could handle the men in the "muscle jobs" dealing with the raw timber, log roll-way, de-barking, and finally the eight-foot high tramway moving the finished lumber to the stacking yard. Charley ostensibly used Lahala as a mill foreman; an obvious distinction that did not set well with the European workers.

*   *   *

By 10 a.m. I had the three vacant boarding rooms cleaned by Ottawa maids. The remaining five rooms were occupied by Chicago tourists. All were spending the month of August traveling the upper Great Lakes' pristine waters and beaches on fashionable passenger steamers fitted with compound engines, in which steam was expanded twice for greater efficiency and speed. The wealthy upper crust viewed prosperous little Aral as an interesting experiment...a successful sawmill with nearly an inexhaustible supply of cheap white pine forests capable of shipping their cargo to Milwaukee, Chicago, and Cleveland. Wright's reputation grew rapidly after 1884 when he took full control of the mill and the forests downstate were being depleted at an alarming rate. Hence the steady flow of lumber buyers, timber-land owners, barge operators, and speculators.

I was certain Wright's visitors had arrived when two men, fully dressed in suits, accompanied by two well-dressed ladies donning sun umbrellas came into town. A distinguished aging black man drove the four-person carriage pulled by two, large, white American Belgian horses. They pulled up in front of the company store and the younger man walked toward me. He was a physically impressive man; six-foot-two, slim yet fit, well dressed, black hair with a full mustache, and dark eyes, narrowed like a predator's considering his surroundings. The other gentleman, similarly dressed, spoke to the driver who gently tapped the horses to move the carriage in front of the boarding house. The women smiled as if amused by my presence.

"Good morning sir. I'm looking for Charles Wright; do you know where I might find him?" The question was polite, respectful yet delivered with a strong sense of authority.

"Yes, he's at the mill, over there." I pointed to the sawmill across the creek. The well dressed man nodded his appreciation, stepped away, stopped and reached in his vest pocket. A long cigar appeared in his mouth as his hand held a burning match to the end and he drew a few deep breaths through the tobacco. He then waved the match out dropping it to the sand and then looked over Aral from the waterside to the west, where Otter Creek met Lake Michigan, and then to the east down the short main street comprising the city center. The horse carriage, along with the driver, remained out in front of the boarding house while the other man went inside, leaving the two ladies under their sun carousals and giggling over something.

Charley must have anticipated their arrival time as he burst from the mill with his collar buttoned, sleeves rolled down ready to greet the distinctive visitor. Charley met the man on the bridge leading to the mill. "Welcome to Aral sir. I'm Charles T. Wright."

"Thank you Mr. Wright. I'm Brad Jackson. I assume you received my telegraph message about our lumber interests...of me and my partners?"

"Yes, I did get your message. Let me take you through the mill and show you the operation...then we can sit down for lunch and discuss your needs." Charley's steel blue eyes and friendly face conveyed an intelligent, pleasant man—quite a contrast from the evening before.

"Very good. That will be fine." The two men walked toward the mill with Charley monopolizing the discussion, frequently pointing to the areas of the lumberyard, including the rollways, belt ramp, the shipping platform and dock area. The tall stranger held a three-inch height advantage over Charles Wright; although Wright's husky stature likely meant he out-weighed Jackson. Lahala had the crew operating at peak performance. Logs were moving down the rollways into the creek. Men tugged, pushed, and hooked the floating logs to move them up the belt ramp, one after the other, while the ripping saw made its "mill music". The steam engine chugged to a fast rhythm and the finished lumber slide down a wet trough tramway from the second level to a team of men stacking and marking the fresh cut planks. As the two men re-appeared on the west end, ground floor level of the mill, the second man accompanying Jackson, exited the boarding house and walked to the mill. He appeared older than Jackson and a bit shorter, walked at a determined pace yet revealing a mild limp in his right leg. His face was weathered, rugged and tan. His full mustache revealed a hint of grey; his hands were wrinkled and rough, clearly suggesting he was a working man, despite his fine clothing. Charley noticed the older man's approach and waved him over with enthusiasm. Jackson removed his cigar from his lips.

"Charles Wright I'd like you to meet Matthew Pullman, my business partner and brother-in-law." Charley beamed with joy, gripped the man's callused hand and shook it vigorously.

"It's nice to meet you Mr. Pullman. Welcome to our little town."

"It's Matt. I like your little town. The boarding house is very welcoming, and the beach looks inviting. I'm sure our wives will tell us all about it. " A hint of a smile broke across Matthew's lips, his eyes softening a bit.

"So you two married sisters...is that right?" Charley was now pouring on the charm, showing real interest in the men and their visit. His face beamed with excitement and his broad smile supported the image.

"Right. I married first, and then Brad caught the attention of the little sister." Both men feigned embarrassment as though they were duped into their marriages. Charley reasoned that the attractive women, even from one-hundred-fifty yards away, were classy, intelligent and used to the finer things in life.

"Matt, would you like a quick tour of the mill before we get together over a light lunch?"

"Thank you but no tour needed. I've studied your operation as we drove in, and I've seen many mills in west Michigan clear down to Muskegon."

The remark told Charley a lot: these men knew the business, they were not passive speculators. Secondly, he sensed they were beginning to get comfortable with him. It was time to move to the "selling phase", having finished the "showing phase" of making the visitors very comfortable. The three-some walked toward the company store where I had set up a porch table for a cold lunch of sandwiches, ice tea, and fruits.

Sara was in her backyard garden selecting some vegetables and plums for later. She noticed me moving between the boarding house and the general store. I waved a "Hello" and she motioned me to join her. I stopped and thought...*do I have time for a chat with my sister...or not?*

"I'm sorry about last night. Charley just had too much to drink again." Sara's expression was one of embarrassment and shame. She was dressed in a light, full length sun dress with a thin scarf around her shoulders and a broad brim straw hat on her head to control her long strawberry blonde hair. Sara was beautiful woman at eighteen and kept a fresh, young look even at her present age of twenty-eight years.

"Sara, I like Charley, you know that, yet he can be a real pain in the butt. Did anything trigger his bad temper last night?"

"Not really. We had a nice dinner at home and he felt like a walk, so we headed toward the company store and those fellows drinking out front seemed to irritate him. He bought me a glass of fruit wine and he had a whiskey. Not ten minutes later that fur trapper began making a lot of noise and Charley started talking to himself about their rude behavior. Next thing I know he confronts the man and beats him for ten minutes."

"Well, one of the other boarders...the Chicago family...left an hour later on the eight-thirty steamer to Glen Haven."

"Anyway I'm having a light lunch prepared for Charley's visitors shortly on the porch of the company store. You want to join them?"

Sara flashed a beautiful, yet timid smile. “No. They will probably have a drink to celebrate if Charley gets them to make a purchase commitment and I don’t want to share in that.”

“Why not, it might keep him in a jolly mood.”

“Actually Fred, I feel that sometimes his wild behavior starts with trying to impress me, which then attracts remarks from observers that he chooses to *put in their place*.”

“You might be right sis...he doesn’t deserve you, ya know.” I smiled at her delicate and caring demeanor, perplexed how she ever fell for Charley.

“I going to walk down the beach for a while and catch some sun.” She smiled, waved goodbye and headed to the water.

CHAPTER--THREE

The plate of sandwiches had just come out to the counter from the store's small kitchen when I noticed Charley and his guests strolling over toward me. Each man enjoyed a freshly rolled cigar courtesy of Charley. The tea pitcher had already been placed on one of the three small porch tables that locals and visitors frequently used to take lunch or enjoy a drink. Charley directed them to the table just as I set the sandwich plate in the center.

"Is there anything else I can get for you Charley?" I tried to support the *friendly town* message to the visitors.

"This looks just fine Fred. Thanks so much. Take a seat fellows."

Charley deliberately took the chair with the poorest view, looking back into the general store, while the two buyers enjoyed a south-westerly view of the Otter Creek, Lake Michigan, and the beach. I then realized the problem—the visitor's wives may also desire lunch. I shot a glance at Charley who instinctively interpreted my look and expression.

"Gentlemen, I apologize. Would your wives like to join us?" Charley adjusted his look to one of concern, mild embarrassment and humility. I stood nearby waiting for instructions.

Both Matt and Brad remained silent for a moment, looked at each other, then to Charley. I felt tension building as I slowly waited for the next words. Both men looked grim and annoyed.

"What do you think Brad...should our wives join us for lunch and discussions with Charley?" I held my breath; Charley froze his eyes on Brad.

Brad carefully spread his cloth napkin across his lap, set aside his hat, removed his half finished cigar then exhaled a string of smoke circles, and said, "Hell no, they'd just be a distraction."

A second passed and Matt and Brad broke into laughter. Charley joined in and said, "Okay!" I allowed myself to breathe again and strolled back inside the store.

"Relax Charley; we never let our wives sit in on these type meetings. They came along for the ride, the beach, and besides they carried a basket lunch from Frankfort to have on the beach. They're fine." The men chuckled as though they had practiced the scene before.

I stood just inside the store and kept an ear tuned into the discussion in case they needed something, yet I didn't want to appear snooping. The lunch selections seemed to go well, with plenty to go around and after a refill of the ice tea pitcher the men settled into serious talk of business.

"Charley, we have twenty-two building contractors down state needing everything from floor beams to finished trim pieces. Our largest contractor in Detroit is Higgins and Brothers. You ever heard of them?"

"Yes, I have but I can't tell you why. Maybe I supplied them." Charley searched his memory to no avail.

"You may have. We own a large lumber yard in Grand Haven and supply the bulk of their requirements but our local suppliers are vanishing...all logged out downstate. Last year we made massive lumber shipments to rebuild the Pingree and Smith Shoe Company after it burned to the ground. Now they want us to supply material to double the plant area. We want to partner with you for shipments *direct* to Pingree around the lake."

"I can handle that for you gentlemen and I'll guarantee on time shipments." Charley conveyed his promise with a calm, smooth delivery, a sincere look, and eyes fixed on his audience, allowing just the hint of a smile.

Matt looked directly into Charley's eyes allowing the tension to build while he formed a response. "We've been down to the Edgewater Mill Charley, and frankly, they don't seem as committed to meet our schedule as you are. If you can match their prices you can have our business for a year. Then we'll both re-access the relationship. Fair enough? Pringree and Smith is a *very important client* for us, and now...*you.* "

For an instant Charley reacted with a rage building inside. The mention of Edgewater, his chief rival in northwest Michigan, provoked the involuntary response. Yet Charley knew he had won them over, which helped control his temper in front of a seasoned pair of serious lumber men serving a huge market downstate. The direct relationship with the shoe manufacturer could expose Charley's Aral operation to the vast

Detroit market. He reacted with just enough excitement to shed any impression that he was expecting to get the order, yet controlled enough to appear professional. It was Charles T. Wright at his best.

"Thanks gentlemen, I won't disappoint you." Charley offered both men a firm handshake to seal the deal, and I knew what was coming next.

"Fred, can you bring out a whiskey bottle and glasses?"

"Of course Charley, I'll be right there." I deliberately grabbed a bottle only half full to discourage more drinking than Charley could manage without reverting to his *mean* side. The next half hour involved several toasts and storytelling.

Charley remained his charming self throughout and as the bottle ran out Sara appeared along with the lumberman's wives. All we're laughing and talking incessantly about their walk, the beach and the basket lunch they had offered to share with Sara. I think my sister has a God given gift to appear at the proper moments and save Charley from himself most times...today was one of those days. Matt and Brad were impressed with Sara and stood to greet her as Charley shone with pride, hugging Sara. She captivated the scene long enough for the wives to insist they stay the night and enjoy a meal at the inn. Matt and Brad feigned resistance and then agreed. I booked them in adjoining rooms with a view of Otter Creek and the beach. Sara discreetly pulled Charley away, walking him toward the mill, before kissing him and heading back to her house.

CHAPTER--FOUR

Sara looked for Charley to return home about six o'clock. Shorty before six the "mill music" stopped and the workers had left for the day. Charley stood outside the mill talking to Lahala when he noticed Sara waving to him.

"I'll be home in a minute honey." Charley looked to the sky and then said something to Lahala before leaving.

Frequently Charley would walk home along the beach, extending his time travel by fifteen minutes but presumably allowing an early evening look at the bay and Lake Michigan to the west. The wind had increased all day from the northwest reaching ten knots for a while. The clue to the end of the day was the melodic wave sounds as they crashed the beach. Charley walked out the largest sand bar, the one he usually fished from, and stood in knee deep water looking down through the crystal clear fresh water. He had made the journey north down the beach some three-hundred yards before stopping at the narrow sandbar. It was a familiar trek for

Charley as he steadfastly made it at least once each week. I never knew why he enjoyed the walk so much, followed by wading around in waist deep water. Yet everyone knew Charley Wright had unusual pleasures as well as strange behaviors. After a few minutes, he would re-appear, moving away from the beach and heading home to Sara, dinner was waiting.

* * *

Jackson and Pullman, along with their wives, enjoyed a nice meal of fish, bread, and vegetables on the porch at the boarding house. My cook did a nice job and the room rental helped cover the loss we incurred when Charley *ran off* the Chicago families through his crazy drunken behavior the night before. The summer was cooler than usual and the typical "dog days" of August were actually pleasant, if one kept the windows open. After dinner the couples took brandies and walked to the mouth of Otter Creek to watch the sunset arrive. The water calmed down and as the sun retreated below the horizon the sky evolved from a dark blue, to orange, to dark red before all that remained were silver blue shimmers of light reflecting off the water and the few scattered clouds faded to pink and then grey. A light was on in the Wright bedroom and I could hear Charley snoring as Sara no doubt tried to read. Smartly, she managed to keep him indoors after dinner and he fell asleep before transforming into the antagonistic Charley Wright. Meanwhile the little town of Aral was swelling with visitors. The nine o'clock ferry from Platte River arrived four minutes early and unloaded four couples and two unaccompanied men. Two couples took the last remaining rooms at the boarding house and the remaining two couples were friends of Dr. Thurber, a local doctor and township treasurer, who was expecting them as house guests for several days. Earlier a larger steamer, the Dewar, anchored off the mill dock to spend the night with sixteen passengers on board in cabins. The general store stayed open till ten o'clock, later than usual, to accommodate the late arrivals. I kept serving drinks and selling merchandise to visitors till I closed up. There was a bustle that lingered in the town that night...I was pleased to know Charley Wright was asleep and not drinking in the streets with the crowd.

*   *   *

The next morning, at dawn, I had my cook prepare breakfast items including eggs, ham, sausage, and biscuits along with hot coffee and tea. By 8:30 a.m. the town was getting back to normal; Wright's lumbermen left early to drive their carriage back to Frankfort to board the afternoon steamer south. The "mill music" started at about 7 a.m. yet Charley was nowhere to be seen. I figured he either went directly to the mill or was still sleeping although he seldom overslept without a previous night of heavy drinking and fighting. As I walked toward the mill I saw Charley coming up from the mouth of the Otter Creek. His pants were wet up past the knees and he carried a small, wet canvas bag. He seemed in a hurry and didn't notice me.

"Catch a few fish this morning Charley?"

He was startled at seeing me and froze in his tracks for an instant. Then he quickly picked up his pace and walked into the mill never looking back.

“Wasn’t fishing...just checked out the dock area for our afternoon shipment.” He disappeared into the mill and looked back at me just as he passed through the door. I shrugged at Charley’s ever changing behavior...some days he couldn’t stop talking playfully...other times he was just rude. Today was starting out as a rude day.

CHAPTER--FIVE

Racine, Wisconsin July 10, 1889

James Wright sat in his single horse carriage sipping a brandy from his pocket flask surveying the Lake Michigan shore. The scene was very familiar, a mild summer evening, the sun dropping lower in the west, and in the distant waters a streamer heading into port. James reflected on the four earlier trips Charley made to Racine from Aral. The 6:30 p.m. steamer rounded the pier and moved slowly to the passenger dock. Charles Wright stood ready to step off the ship when he spotted the familiar carriage and waved to his brother. Ten minutes later Charley humped his ruck sack over his right shoulder and marched to James.

"Hi Charley, smooth, calm waters I assume."

"Yeah, and we made good time with a steady, mild northwest wind." Charley slung his sack behind the bench seat on the carriage.

"Care for a little nip before dinner?" James passed the leather covered flask to his brother. Charley unscrewed the cap, pulled the cork, and threw back a swallow of the smooth liquor.

"I found some more gold pieces...eighteen of them." Charley reached in his pocket and removed a small canvas bag which he shook to slide the shiny twenty dollar gold coins into his hand. The bright coins brought back a significant memory to both men.

Among the items their Uncle Joe left upon his death was an old, oil-skin, caped trench coat. The one he escaped the Westmoreland in when it sank off South Manitou Island. Days after Joe's death, Charley felt something in a side pocket—six twenty-dollar gold coins wrapped in a hand note stating: *Treasure from the Westmoreland, washed into my coat pockets as whiskey barrels shattered as the ship broke up. Joseph Wright, December 9, 1854.* The note and coins explained to the brothers, their uncle's story and his final cryptic remarks just minutes before he passed away.

"I think that makes more than nine hundred you've found... about $18,000." James snapped the straps and the horse lurched forward pulling away from the dock.

"Right. Every time a northwest wind exceeds, say seven knots for a day, more gold shows up. It gets moved along the northern side of the sand bar near Otter Creek."

"Has anyone discovered what you're doing out on that sand bar?" James looked directly at his brother.

"No, not so far. Sara doesn't even know... not yet... I'm afraid she might fail to keep the secret. Her brother Fred is a problem; he watches the town like a hawk yet still doesn't know anything. He thinks I love to fish."

James chuckled at his brother's chicanery. Charley took another long swallow and corked the flask. "Every summer a batch of treasure hunters arrive and prowl the shoreline from Frankfort to Leland...some have heard the rumor about the Westmoreland gold. We need it to remain a *rumor* until we can buy Edgewater and then control all the lumber harvesting in northwest Michigan for the next ten years."

Charley took another hit of brandy, corked and then capped the flask, handing it back to James. "Then I can buy out Helen Davis completely."

"Davis...I thought you paid O'Leary?"

"O'Leary sold the lease to her last year after he expanded the mill, No matter, I send him the payment and he forwards it on to her. If we had this pile of gold coins back then I'd be done with the lease payment."

"Soon, my brother, soon."

* * *

The brothers drove the carriage a few blocks into town and found their favorite pub — O'Banyon's. The place was a haunt for sailors, dock workers, warehousemen and the occasional businessman. The food was marginal, brown, hot and greasy yet the cozy pub was always lively with an Irish tenor singing off in a far corner. James and Charles sat near the bar at a small table. The Guinness and shots flowed before, during, and after the bangers and mash meals both men ordered. The discussion grew robust and loud through dinner, and by the shank of the evening both men were drunk. James and Charley however were complete opposite's — James the happy drunk, Charley the aggressive drunk. Both men were hard workers and smart businessmen, yet the younger, James, had a discipline and analytical side which preceded his every action. Charles however, was spontaneous and intuitive in his approach to life. In business he had been lucky to have James to provide a reflective view on their decisions concerning the Racine mill operation. James sensed the pub crowd was taking too much interest in their discussion, which drifted in and out of their financial good fortune. Two rough looking sailors stood at the bar rail and had watched the brothers carry on. James took notice and leaned in to whisper to Charley.

"Let's get on home brother...this place may have ears."

"What ...who...?" James instinctively glanced at the two sailors. Charley caught the two in his sight and stood up before them.

"Charley come on...let's go home." James feared the worst.

"You guys got sometin' to say to us?" The two men sipped their beers and smirked at Charley's sloppy speech. The larger man, in his thirties, was close to six-foot-two and very muscular.

"We just were wondering if you're a braggart or a liar mate." The rugged man tipped his beer mug up and half emptied it. He stared at Charley, sizing him up.

Charley vaulted into action, grabbing the smaller man by the belt and throwing him to the floor after crashing into the brothers' table. The larger man swung his drink hand, still holding the mug of beer at Charley's head and caught him in the temple. Charley staggered back, just as James stood to help steady his brother and said, "Come on...we gotta go now."

Charley held his head as the larger man advanced to deliver a punishing downward blow with his other hand.
A vicious upper cut from Charley's right hand caught the big man in the belly, bending him over. He then followed up with two more blows to the man's head, ripping his nose open and cracking his jaw bone. A second later, the smaller man ran at Charley slamming him into the bar rail. James grabbed the smaller man and pulled him off Charley, but not before

Charley landed three fast blows, left, right, left, dropping the man into a bloody heap on the floor before James. The larger man regained his feet and charged toward Charley, who stepped aside and delivered a crushing blow to the man's neck, bending him over in pain. As he turned and straightened up Charley unleashed a flurry of blows to the man's chest, face and belly, sending him to the floor again.

"Damnit Charley, let's go!!" He pulled Charley by his suspenders out the door and down the street to their waiting carriage.

James struck a match, held it to Charley's head and saw a three-inch gash running from his hair line down near his left temple. "Damn, Charley, you may need stitches for this one. Why did you have to pick a fight anyhow?"

"I didn't like the way they was lookin' at us...like we was scum or somethin'...why?"

"We got too much going for us to mess up beating some old salts to death."

Charley held his shirt sleeve to his bloody head and looked at James who had slapped the horse to pull away from the tie-rail.

“Yeah, I guess I know you’re right...sorry.”

James glanced at his brother, looked back at O’Banyon’s for any lingering trouble, and remarked, “It’s alright, I guess they didn’t die... you damn fearless fool.” A smile ran across his face as he studied his brother.

* * *

The next morning Charley Wright examined his bruised head and bloody knuckles as he waited for the last kettle of heated water James’ son’s, Chester, lugged to the bathroom tub. The timid twelve-year old, was slim and tall, yet strong, easily pouring the heavy steaming water bucket into the tub and avoiding any eye contact with his uncle. Charley studied the lad and as he left said, “Thanks Chester, you’re a good boy.”

Chester looked back briefly, again avoiding eye contact and replied, “Your welcome sir.”

Charles T. Wright longed for a family like his brother had...a loving wife, two kids, Chester and Sally, and a nice home. The lumber business James and Charley inherited in their early twenties when their father died prematurely provided a nice income...for one man and his family. Charley was looking for an opportunity to acquire his own operation and grow it with help from James. The lumber mill in Aral Michigan provided the ideal answer, with a passive owner, O'Leary, seeking a manager three years earlier, and now the ability to own the mill through a lease. His discovery of the Westmoreland gold confirmed the rumors and stories were true, despite several failed attempts by salvage teams to recover the *treasure*. The map Joseph Wright left his nephews, while not scaled was incredibly accurate as to the relative location of the sinking, South Manitou, and Sleeping Bear Point. When overlaid with the prevailing northwest wind grid the long, shallow sandbar near Otter Creek was a logical spot to find the gold pieces. After several failed searches, Charley Wright discovered a string of sixteen coins, dispersed over fifteen feet, caressing the north side of the bar after a strong, sustained over night wind. That day he began a secret campaign, along with his brother James, to recover sufficient gold to fund the purchase of the Aral and Edgewater lumber mills.

During the summer months of 1888 and 1889, Charley Wright made eleven early morning trips to the sand bar and collected the gold coins following a blowing northwest wind during the night. Returning from the beach Charley made certain he was not followed or seen as he hid the treasure in a small canvas bag beneath a loose floorboard on his rear porch. Periodically Charley took a day journey by schooner to Racine, met with James who stockpiled the coins in a safety deposit box, and then returned to Aral two days later. The gold value had grown to a point which, when added to the mill profits, meant Charley could buy out O'Leary/Davis from the lease. Once the Aral mill was free of lease debt Charley could turn his sights to Edgewater and when acquired, control the lumber markets in northwest Michigan.

CHAPTER--SIX

Aral Michigan, July 31, 1889

I was pleased the weather had returned to the balmy, warm, sunny days that the two weeks following a full moon in late July typically produced. A nasty wind and cold front from the northwest spoiled two days last week resulting in less carriage and steamer traffic. I looked for Charley to tell him my good news. The mill music had started two hours earlier yet Charley was not around. I decided to stroll around town and head towards the river mouth. As I stood on the fore dune and looked out at the gentle rolling waves, now diminished greatly from the winds of last evening, I noticed a person standing in the water several hundred yards away. At first, I thought it was one of the Ottawa Indian women washing, yet as I moved to get a better view it was clearly a man. It looked at little like Charley, yet the man wasn't fishing, merely standing and occasionally reaching down into the water. The man began moving towards shore and I lost sight of him as the dune grass hid him from my view. As I walked away and passed over the small dune I looked back and saw another man with binoculars kneeling in the grass scanning the water to the west. My curiosity waned, so I decided to return to the boarding house and check the mill again for Charley.

At 8:30 a.m. Charley came wandering in from the beach; his pants soaking wet. "You been fishing again Charley?" I noticed he carried no pole or fish stringer.

"Yeah, I thought I might get lucky, but no bites." Charley's smile revealed a happy disposition.

I struggled for an instant if he was the man I saw north of Otter Creek, or not. Dismissing the notion I said, "Well, here's some good news. The boarding house has full bookings well into September—better than last year."

"That's great Fred. Do you need more supplies or help to manage the tourist crowd?"

"Man, you are feeling good... it's not often you *offer* to stock my shelves."

"Well damnit Fred, I do feel good and the mill's doing well, so let's stock up for the fall crowds."

Charley waved as he walked on towards his house, his wet jeans still dripping from his early morning fishing attempt. I hoped his friendly disposition continues into the evening.

* * *

Charley Wright could not control his joy. Near his rear porch, hidden from view he removed his wet jeans and dumped eighty-one twenty dollar gold pieces on the sand. It was the largest single cache recovered from the Westmoreland he had made in two years. He then stored the coins in a canvas sack. He couldn't help but speculate how he and James would re-structure the lumber business in northwest Michigan. It was all possible now with the Westmoreland gold. He was ready to buy out O'Leary's lease. The Aral mill would soon be his—free and clear. Edgewater was next.

* * *

The Aral Mill Company Store

I had just completed an order list for my handyman, Eddy, before he headed to Frankfort for supplies. As he left, Dr. Frank Thurber walked in and sat at a table with another man who looked familiar. Later, I recognized him as someone associated with the Edgewater Mill on the Platte River.

I liked Dr. Frank Thurber, a practicing physician and Lake Township Treasurer, who lived in Aral and managed to play an active role in local politics. The rush of jobs and lumber buyers to the Otter Creek area together with travelers seeking the restful summer weather along Lake Michigan's shore kept the shop keepers, fishermen, and inn keepers busy. Charley Wright benefitted from a perfect blend of economic growth, depleted forests downstate, and available local labor. His business touch seemed mystical yet his reckless personal behavior sometimes overshadowed his commercial success. Nevertheless, Dr. Frank Thurber was not impressed with Wright and I frequently heard him comment on Charley's crude, loud mouth antics. Thurber felt Wright was not a true genius at business; rather more of a lucky lumberjack who got his way with a "gift-of-gab" and a force of personality. The one contra indictor to Thurber's opinion was Sara, my sister, Wright's wife, who by all accounts was a beautiful, caring, sensitive woman devoted to the man.

Frank Thurber also saw the potential for fortunes to be made in the white pine lumber business; and had hoped O'Leary might consider an investment by him, but only if Wright were fired. O'Leary held Wright in high regard solely based on his financial performance at the mill. The investment offer by Thurber fell on deaf ears, which caused the determined doctor to look for other avenues to derail Charles T. Wright. Reflecting on all this made me curious about the seemingly serious meeting Thurber was having with the man from Edgewater.

CHAPTER--SEVEN

Benzonia, Michigan, Sheriff's Office, August 9, 1889

At precisely 11:59 a.m. Sheriff Case flipped the cardboard sign showing "Closed" for all visitors to see. He wanted a quiet, private place to discuss his business with Dr. Frank Thurber and Deputy Neil Marshall. He entered his small office, shut the door, stirred sugar into his coffee, and looked at the two men. "Tell me what you propose doctor."

"We all know Charles Wright has not paid his taxes in over a year and we need to collect what's due the county. If we delay we invite others to test our resolve. My role as County treasurer compels me to act." Thurber looked pleased at his own remarks.

"You have a writ prepared for me to approve Neil?" The sheriff looked curiously at Thurber.

"Yes, sir, here it is. The writ attaches the logs Wright has dammed in Otter Creek as payment for delinquent taxes."

Sheriff Case glanced at the writ and asked, "What does Wright have to say about this?"

Thurber reacted immediately. "He has been non-responsive to our notices."

Marshall questioned, "Didn't he object to the fast rise in his tax bill last year?" Marshall tried to not agitate Thurber who issued the tax bill.

Thurber shot a glance at Marshall and replied, "His mill is expanded, recently rebuilt and is doing very well. The tax is fair."

Case held his steaming coffee just below his mustache breathing in the warm fumes as he spoke, "Then if the tax is due and he has not disputed it formally, I'll sign the writ." Thurber's face revealed a tight grin as his eyes flashed confidence.

"Thank you sheriff, we'll issue this personally tomorrow." Marshall collected the signed writ and nodded to Thurber.

Dr. Frank Thurber fitted his hat to his head and smiled. "You've done the right thing Sheriff Case. Thank you."

Sheriff Case studied the passionate words of the doctor and wondered if he truly had done the *right thing*.

* * *

The evening air was cool, fresh, and pleasant due to the clear sky and a mild northwest wind. The Frankfort ferry arrived at six o'clock sharp and deposited fourteen people in the little town of Aral. Two boats anchored off the mill dock and seven men came in for supplies and drinks. One boat was setup for commercial fishing and the other appeared to be salvage barge, resembling a tug. Charley arrived after dinner with Sara and strolled by the company store porch. He had been drinking but was happy and holding Sara's hand as they slowly walked around town.

"Good evening Fred. Looks like your boarding house is full." Charley was at the talkative stage in his drinking and Sara appeared to have control of him.

"Yes sir, we are full. We have a nice bunch of folks in town." My sister caught my veiled warning to Charley to not screw up the evening.

"We'll see you later Fred. Sara and I are gonna catch the sunset and then stop by for a wee drink before turning in." Sara whispered something to Charley which made him blush, just as she pulled him away towards the beach. I waved a goodbye hoping Sara's plan was to take him home directly, bypassing the drink.

Charley and Sara made their way to beach, walked north a couple of hundred yards, and sat on an old, white-washed, driftwood tree trunk partially buried in the sand. It made for a comfortable spot to relax and watch the approaching sunset. The scene appearing over the calm waters of Otter Bay as the encroaching sunset was incredible. Brilliant reds and orange hues spread across the sky just above the horizon, and extended from the near end of South Manitou to the open water west of Frankfort. Charley sat close to Sara and hugged her briefly as though he were preparing to say something. The couple held hands and watched the panorama of color strengthen as the sun fell near the skyline. Sara sensed a strange, relaxed mood in her husband of almost five years and decided to raise a taboo subject.

"Charley I want to have a baby. We've tried and tried yet I've never gotten pregnant. Dr. Thurber has examined me and says that there's no reason I cannot conceive. Won't you please make your appointment and see if there's a reason we can't conceive a child?"

Charley initially reacted in his typical manner thinking...*what there's nothing wrong with me...it can't be me.* Looking directly into Sara's eyes he could see her love and concern for him which helped control his tendency to erupt in a defensive retort. She seemed radiant in the low sunlight and kept her focus on Charley with and expectant smile across her lips. He then had the good sense to pause, reflect and think through his next words.

"Sara, you know how much you mean to me...and there is nothin' I wouldn't do to make you happy. But, I don't like Thurber and don't trust him."

Sara's saddening face told Charley he had not settled the issue; he felt an impulse to tell her about his good fortune in the Westmoreland gold find. He looked at her and held her hand. "I want to share something very special with you...something that will change our lives forever and make all your concerns go away."

Sara's face relaxed and a smile began to spread once more across her lips. Charley turned to her and began, "You've met my brother James from Racine. Well he and I have been on a search for something our father and uncle pursued for over twenty years. I've now found it and...."

Charley's face twisted to a grim look of anger, his muscles tensed and he stared out to the water. He stood abruptly and shaded his eyes from the lowering sun to see something. Sara sat baffled as Charley stood and looked north.

"Charley what's the matter...are you alright...talk to me?" Sara looked out at the water, confused and frightened.

"Stay here ...do not follow me!" Charley jumped back behind the fore dune and began to sprint north along the shore towards the sand bar. Sara watched in amazement at the strange behavior from her husband. Then Charley appeared in the distance and ran toward the water, jumped over the fore dune, and lunged to the shoreline. Sara moved to see over the dune grass and saw Charley wrestling with a man who had just come in from the water's edge.

"What are you doing here...what are you looking for?" Charley slammed a fist into the startled man's face crushing his cheek bone and ripping his left eye brow. The man said nothing for a moment then smiled, "You're Charley Wright, ain't you? I think I know what you been up to."

Charley screamed a wild yell as he leapt toward the man again. This time a fist fight ensued but the man, close to Charley's size and age, defended himself with skill and hammered Charley back with three successive blows to the face and belly, sending him to the ground. Charley retaliated with a butting blow to the chest of the man and drove him into the water. Charley went into a full-out assault on the man, now handicapped in the water, and landed several crushing blows the head of the stunned man. He lay semi-conscious in a foot of water as Charley backed off and looked down the beach. Two hundred yards south was Sara, crying, on her knees, unable to explain Charley's behavior.

Charley looked the man over; he'd seen him before in meetings with Dr. Thurber in town and realized he was probably a fortune hunter hired by Thurber to spy on his activities out on the sand bar. In a desperate move, Charley surveyed the surrounding area for any of the twenty dollar gold pieces, then pulled the man ashore and checked his pockets...nothing appeared. For a moment Charley considered pushing the man out into deeper water where he might drown; but instead decided to make his point more personal. He grabbed the man by the lapels and shook him alert. Starring intensely into the man's bloody face Charley warned, "If I see you out here again, you'll never walk the beach anymore. Understand? Get outta here!"

The man nodded almost involuntarily at the deadly threat and slumped back down in the wet sand. Charley wiped his face on his sleeve and began walking back to Sara. His mind raced with thoughts on how to explain his reaction to seeing a man on the sand bar and attacking him for no apparent reason; nothing came to mind and as he re-joined Sara, he simply remarked, "Sorry, I'll explain later." The tears streamed down Sara's cheeks.

*　　*　　*

The late evening did produce a brilliant sunset to compliment a pleasant cooling breeze, yet I never did see Charley and Sara return for that drink. I was just as happy to believe that she was successful in her whispered remark to lure Charley home to bed...rather than provoking a fight in town.

As I finally closed up the bar service at the company store, I noticed the lights in Charley's house were dark, a good sign. Little did I know life in Aral was about to change in ways no one could imagine. No one.

CHAPTER--EIGHT

Aral Michigan, Morning, August 10, 1889

The morning "mill music" began on schedule announcing the 7:00 a.m. start to mill operations. Another beautiful August summer day at Otter Bay was underway. I was sweeping off the company store porch as usual when I noticed Charley leaving his front door and heading to the mill. I stopped sweeping expecting to exchange our typical daybreak chatter yet Charley kept his head down and marched directly to the mill bridge. Strange I thought...particularly since Charley loved to talk, didn't make a nuisance of himself in town the night before, and was therefore freed from explaining his bad behavior. I reasoned Sara may provide some clues later in the day.

By nine o'clock the town was bustling with activity. The boarding house crowd made their way out for breakfast at the porch at my company store and the sleep-over passengers on board the Frankfort ferry made their way into town. The day was starting out as a perfect summer day, comfortable temperatures, no rain expected, billowy clouds drifting in from the northwest and lots of tourists. Just before ten o'clock, Dr. Thurber appeared in the street walking from his nearby home. He looked fidgety and angry, something was bothering him. He saw me and strolled up, hands on his hips. "Fred, have you seen Wright yet this morning?"

"Yeah, he walked over to the mill about seven."

"Did he say anything to you about last night?" Thurber's face had the look of a predator.

"Actually no. He never looked my way... rather unusual. Why?" I waited for Thurber to fill me in on Charley's foul demeanor. He didn't. Instead he lit a slim cigar and drew in a long breath before he spoke.

"I'll talk to you later Fred." He walked to the edge of town near where the road to Benzonia started.

* * *

The mill had operated at near peak capacity for almost two months. Downstate lumber buyers came regularly, inspected the mill, negotiated with Charley, occasionally stayed the night, bought meals and drinks. The town felt alive and vibrant with all the activity, visitors and great weather. I sat down to take a break from the morning rush of buyers seeking dry goods and house supplies. The sun tea looked ready so I poured a glass, added ice and sat down on the porch. That's when I noticed trouble.

He rode a single horse drawn carriage, a 12-gauge shotgun strapped to the side board behind the whip sleeve. He was a tall man, six-foot-six inches tall, heavy set, muscular and donned a full, dark chin beard. He stopped near the mill bridge as Dr. Thurber appeared and spoke to the man. They exchanged a few words, pointing to the mill, then the company store. I felt a strange chill come over me as Thurber jumped in the carriage and they looked over my way. I stood up involuntarily as the men approached.

"Fred, this is Deputy Neil Marshall from Benzonia. We need a quiet place to talk for a few minutes."

The big man towered above me, looking very intimidating, yet relaxed me when he smiled and said, "Hello Fred, pleased to meet you."

"I'm pleased to meet you deputy. Ahh... take this table right here, I was just leaving to go ... in the store for...inventory sorting." I felt my stupid remark failed to hide my insecurity. Thurber looked to me, motioned with his head to "get lost" and I promptly left.

* * *

Lahala got the mill crew working at full speed minutes after they stoked the boiler up to high fire and started the big saw. Minutes later Charley arrived and Lahala motioned to him.

"You look troubled boss... you have a bad night drinking?" Charley refused to comment on the insights of his top foreman. He motioned Lahala over near his office desk, tucked in a corner of the boiler room.

"Have your Indian scouts learned anything about the writ talk?" Charley slurped a cup of hot, strong, black coffee as he studied Lahala's reaction.

Lahala scanned the work crew for listeners. "Sheriff Case met with doc and his deputy yesterday morning. Looks like they got the writ to hand you today...deputy to arrive at ten this morning. What you wanna do boss?"

"Keep the mill running regardless of what they try. I'll deal with the damn crooks, trying to tax me out of business."

Charley opened a small drawer in his cluttered desk and retrieved a pocket flask. He poured a long shot into the coffee mug and capped the flask.

"You need me out with you when they come boss?"

Lahala respected Charles Wright, and Charley respected Lahala. It was a friendship based on keeping promises. Lahala promised to keep the mill running smoothly, even when the Polish, German and Finlanders resented Lahala's elevated role at the mill. Charley promised to keep Lahala working, paying him a fair wage, and confiding in him.

"I have plenty of reasons to deal with Thurber. Today's as good a day as any...right?" Charley uncapped his flask once again and took a long mouthful in as Lahala watched.

"Don't be gettin' drunk when you need to be smart boss. Deputy is a big, mean looking man." Lahala sensed his boss was heading to a critical time ... a time where all their fates could change...for the worse.

"Relax, I can handle this." The booze was tempting the reckless, volatile side of Charles T. Wright to appear.

CHAPTER--NINE

Aral Lumber Mill, August 10, 1889

I knew trouble was brewing when Dr. Thurber stood with the giant of a man, in Deputy Marshall, and pointed to the mill entrance. The big man walked over the Otter Creek Bridge as Wright and Lahala were organizing a team to man the log rollway and drop fresh logs in the water for processing. Charley must have expected the deputy's arrival since when he came out from the mill he carried his favorite weapon, a Marlin 30-30 lever action. I could feel the tension building as Charley became very distressed and swore at the deputy several times, threatening to "drop you where you stand" if he didn't leave the property.

"I'm Deputy Neil Marshall and I'm here to enforce a valid writ of attachment on your log inventory for nonpayment of taxes. Now stop the log rolling." Marshall became very agitated.

Several times the men shouted orders to the workers: Marshall ordering them to stop the log rolling, and Charley yelling for them to continue working. Lahala kept the workers operating the mill and prompted compliance with the log rolling every time Charley screamed his demands.

After an extended back-and-forth confrontation, Deputy Marshall said, "You think about your actions real careful Wright... or I'll arrest you and shut you down today."

Charley just glared at the big man and held tight to his 30-30. Marshall said he would have lunch and give Charley a chance "to cool down" before he came back to enforce the writ.

Charley and Lahala again ordered the workers to continue log rolling and sawing operations despite what Marshall said. Charley went back to the mill and finished the remaining whiskey in his flask. The anger boiled in Charley's head. He was so close to having the mill "purchase" cash and then over the last few months his tax bill jumped to an excessive level leaving him short the cash needed to buy out the lease. He felt Thurber was trying to deny him the opportunity to own the mill outright...perhaps to allow his Edgewater buddies to take over along with him. His mind replayed the events of late emboldening his suspicions of Thurber...the rage increased with the help of the booze.

Noon had a come and gone. Lahala came to the company store and said, "Boss wants another bottle of whiskey. He said don't worry."

I hesitated and Lahala remarked, "I can talk him into calming down...but not if he thinks I disobeyed his order. Give me a bottle..."

Lahala had a special skill, seldom seen in other Ottawa Indians, to understand the white man and work with them...in particular, the white man named Charley Wright. I thought hard and long and finally agreed, "Here it is. I hope you can get through to him. He can get very bull-headed you know."

"I know...but I can talk to him."

The calm, confident, and intelligent Lahala took the whiskey bottle and walked back to the mill. Thurber and Deputy Marshall were on the company store porch having an intense discussion before their lunch order arrived. It was just after 1:30 p.m. and the mill was still operating at full tilt. Most workers assumed the fracas was over yet Lahala knew the real trouble lay ahead. Charley Wright was in the blacksmith shop barking out orders on a repair needed on the saw carriage. Lahala found him and motioned for Charley to meet him at his desk area.

"Boss, that deputy and doc are having a lunch across the river and they will be back. You need to hear them out and work a deal to keep the mill open, Right?"

Charley grabbed the whiskey bottle and unscrewed the cap, took a hard look at Lahala and slung the bottle to his mouth, depleting a quarter of the liquid in a single swallow.

"I need to show them they can't push me around. That big tax bill is just Thurber's plan to force me out...so he can take over! He doesn't know who he's messin' with."

"Yeah boss he *does* know you...and he'll have the sheriff department arrest you if you don't play along. Can't keep the mill goin' if you're locked up."

"I'm bettin' they'll leave after this morning's brush-up and come back in a month or so. I could work a deal by then...maybe."

Lahala tried to encourage the moderation Charley displayed and offered, "Right boss. That's what you need to do, calm down and play for time. We can work this out."

Charley's back stiffened after he took another hit on the whiskey bottle. "Oh, I'll stay calm alright...but they better not push me."

Charley opened his bottom desk drawer and retriever a 32-caliber, six shot revolver, spun the cylinder to make certain all six rounds were loaded, and snapped it shut, dropping it into his vest pocket.

Lahala looked out the small window nearby Charley's desk and saw Thurber and Marshall walking to the bridge across Otter Creek. Charley took notice and looked out at the two men marching toward the mill. Looking back at Lahala, Charley smiled, grabbed his Marlin rifle, racked in a 30-30 round and remarked, "I guess they'd rather talk than go home. Stay in the mill Lahala."

Thurber and Marshall were met in the middle of the bridge. Charley stood defiantly in their way and declared, "Stay off my mill site. This is your last warning." He held the 30-30 at hip level, one hand on the barrel the other on the trigger and lever arm.

Thurber held his arm in front of the big deputy and halted their advance. "Charley, we have a valid writ of attachment for unpaid taxes, we intend to shut you down and take over the log inventory." Thurber held up the signed writ.

"I don't care. You've been trying to shut me down all along. This ginned up tax bill is just your latest gimmick. Now get the hell outta here."

Deputy Neil Marshall quickly became enraged and moved closer to Charley.

"You will shut down or I will arrest you now. Is that clear Mr. Wright?" Marshall reached for his handcuffs or a weapon, and Charley raised his rifle. Marshall was able to grab the rifle barrel and began to tussle for control of the weapon. Charley swung his arms back and forth, and jerked the rifle away from Marshall's grip. At that point Marshall lunged forward to grab the rifle again, but Charley was too quick. He raised the 30-30 to shoulder level, aimed at the deputy's head and fired. The round caught the big man in the forehead, shattering the back of his head. He dropped to his knees, blood running down his face, eyes still open, and then fell face down, dead in the dirt.

Thurber stood in a state-of-shock unable to believe the scene before him. He ran and tackled Charley knocking him to ground, struggling for the rifle. The workers at the log roll, heard the shot, stopped working and looked in amazement at the struggle. The mill workers halted production and stared at the scene on the bridge. Others in town turned to see the ruckus taking place on the bridge. After a minute or so, Charley released his grip on the rifle and Thurber held it in his hands. Both men stood up, exhausted, only a few yards apart. In a flash, Charley reached in his vest pocket for the 32, held it in his outstretched right hand, aimed at Thurber's head and fired. The bullet caught Thurber in the left forehead area, near the temple. He spun around in pain, dropping the rifle, clutching his head. Charley picked up the Marlin 30-30, racked in another shell, took aim at Thurber and fired a lethal round into his chest, he died in seconds. Charley Wright calmly looked at his handy work, scanned the town and mill yard for onlookers and walked back into the mill. Moments later the mill music started again.

* * *

Word of the shooting spread through little Aral in minutes. I watched the entire encounter from the company store after Thurber and Marshall finished lunch and headed to the mill to enforce the writ. My emotions ran wild: Charley shot two men; was it in self defense; whose pistol was involved, Charley's or Thurber's; my sister husband is a killer.

I finally decided someone needed to check on the two men laying on the bridge—were they alive or dead. I found myself wondering if Charley Wright had gone crazy and would shoot me if I intervened. Nevertheless, something had to be done. I stepped out onto the street and two other onlookers followed me to the bridge. It was clear, as I approached, both men were dead. I looked for Charley and Lahala said he was not in the mill yard. The town was in shock, so much so that it was an hour before anyone thought to alert the Benzonia sheriff's office of the tragedy. Two visiting couples used their wives carousals to cover the bodies from the hot summer sun. A single rider ran his horse to alert Sheriff A.B. Case, who reportedly was meeting with officials in Empire.

I looked for Sara and could not find her at home. I worried that she was not safe...Charley Wright was nowhere in sight.

CHAPTER--TEN

Aral, Michigan, Late Afternoon, August 10, 1889

I managed to calm the small crowd of visitors in Aral that the trouble had passed and the authorities were being alerted. I then went to the small telegraph station set up near my desk in the company store. I tapped in the message to Benzonia Prosecuting Attorney, George Covell: *Two men murdered in Main Street Aral, Dr. Frank Thurber and Deputy Neil Marshall. Conflict arose between Charles T. Wright, Aral Mill operator, and the deceased over a writ of attachment. Wright escaped. Send coroner and sheriff.*

The rider caught up with Sheriff Case as he was leaving Empire on his way back to Benzonia. Later that day, Case and Prosecutor Covell, accompanied by the local newspaper editor and photographer, left from Frankfort for Aral on the steamer Dewar. Accompanying them was a twenty-man posse that arrived just as the sun was setting and a full moon was rising.

Without being seen by anyone in town, including me, Charley reportedly returned to the mill later in the afternoon and had Lahala shut down the operation and send the workers home. I kept searching for my sister until dark but she was nowhere to be seen. I feared the worst.

The sheriff quickly took charge. He sent the posse to each end of the town in search for Charley, yet he was not found. The crowd grew to a few dozen people, mostly locals, some visitors, and several disgruntled workers. Torches were lit near the crime scene and the photographer took dozens of pictures at the instruction of attorney Covell. A frenzy started as the sheriff spoke to eyewitnesses, including a mill worker, Abel, a Swedish immigrant with adequate English skills.

"Where were you when the conflict started, Abel?" The sheriff had a junior officer taking notes of the questioning. Another held a torch above the sheriff.

"I work the log rolls. I was there watchin' the men with Charley Wright." Abel pointed to the log roll area, thirty yards away.

"What did you see?" Abel pulled his hat off and took a deep breath.

"When the men came over the second time, Charley got real mad. He had a rifle in his hand too. He said, 'leave or I'll drop you'."

"Who started the fight?" Several workers, under Lahala's supervision, yelled out an answer. Two men stationed near the bridge by Lahala, McCormick and Peck, spoke up with passion.

"Charley killed them. He was drunk and Lahala gave him whiskey. Lahala knows where he is..." The sheriff warned to be crowd to be quiet, touching his sidearm to make the point.

Lahala stood in the background, listening, yet saying nothing. He felt many eyes turning to him. These were the same men he managed skillfully each day in running the mill. They were jealous and ready to use the tragedy to point a critical finger at Lahala—a friend and accomplice to Charley's escape. The prosecutor said, "Lahala are you here... show yourself." The sheriff first noticed the Indian's movement from the rear of the crowd.

The crowd erupted, "He's here, right there!" A dozen fingers angrily pointed out the Ottawa Indian. Lahala said nothing as he walked into the torch light's glow and stood before the prosecutor.

"Are you Lahala?" The prosecutor spoke with a serious voice removing all thought of lying to him. The sheriff stood alongside with his hand resting on his 38-caliber revolver.

"Yes, I am Lahala."

"You work for Charley Wright at the mill...is that correct?" The crowd buzzed again with insults and racial slurs as Lahala prepared to answer the question. "What is your job?"

"Yes I work for boss Charley. I am foreman." The sheriff raised his hand and glared at the noisy crowd.

"Do you know where Charles Wright is hiding?" The crowd erupted again, spewing accusing words of protecting

Charley. The sheriff pulled his revolver and fired a shot in the air, silencing the mob.

"No, I don't know where he is...he left around 4 o'clock...didn't say anything to me."

"Liar, you're covering for him..." Abel couldn't believe he let his thought become word.

"I'm sorry...I'll be quiet." Abel slid back into the crowd out of sight. The sheriff was losing patience and did not like the answer Lahala offered.

"Bring him down near the water...and get me a rope. We'll find out what this redskin knows." The mob broke into cheers and yells as the posse took Lahala toward the tall tree at the mouth of the creek. I was prodded by a dozen workers, who I knew well, to "fetch a rope from the store". Fearful of becoming their next target I brought a fifty-foot rope to the old oak tree. Several of the posse threw the rope over a limb, fifteen feet up in the air, and created a noose around Lahala's neck. The sheriff now playing to the mob took control of the next scene.

"String him up." The blood thirsty crowd grew intoxicated at the prospect of Lahala's death.

Lahala left the ground in a second, twisting and gasping with his hands tied behind him. The sheriff let him hang six feet above the sand for over a minute before he asked, "Ready to talk?"

Lahala fell hard to ground as the rope was released. He coughed and sputtered, "I don't know where he is... he just left."

"Pull him up again," ordered Sheriff Case. A few in the crowd threw rocks at the twisting Indian now nearly unconscious.

Finally the prosecutor said, "If he dies we'll never learn what he knows." Another minute or more dragged on and Lahala was barely moving when he dropped to the ground a second time. The sheriff took no mention of the prosecutors warning.

"Ready to talk now?" Lahala could do no more than nod his head *"no"* before the rope tightened a third time and he flew up off the ground as the noose tightened more and more around his raw neck. The Indian hung lifeless for thirty seconds, as the crowd watched in expectation of Lahala's death. The sheriff motioned and deputies dropped him down once more. The lifeless Lahala lay unconscious on the ground until a posse member threw a bucket of cold river water on his face. In a spontaneous reaction Lahala woke, coughed, and gagged as he rolled onto his side. The newly sworn posse deputies lifted him before Sheriff Case who now held a whip in his right hand.

"Lahala...last chance, where is Charles Wright?"

The weakened Indian raised his head and lied, "I think he's in the forest north of town."

The sheriff looked at the posse leader, pointed to the woods, and decried, "Split your men by a half-mile either side, of a line five-hundred yards north of right here. Flush him out."

The posse organized themselves into two groups all on horseback, ready to ride out, all heavily armed with guns and kerosene lanterns to drive Charley Wright from his hiding place.

The sheriff looked at the weakened Lahala, then to the prosecutor, before barking one last instruction. "If he resists, shoot to wound. If he fires back, shoot to kill." The crowd cheered their approval.

CHAPTER—ELEVEN

Forest Area North of Aral, Michigan

The raucous crowd noise cut through the cool evening air and told Charley Wright his fate was sealed. He could hear, even at a distance, the sheriff's penetrating voice and feared his friend and confidant Lahala was being tortured and may die any moment. The twenty-man posse advanced to the either side of Charley's position. He hid in a dense cluster of boxwood three-hundred yards north of Aral. He had left the mill hours earlier, met briefly with Sara to give some very specific instructions should he die. She pleaded with him to stay in town and surrender to authorities, yet Charley felt his destiny was sealed the instant he fired on Deputy Marshall, and followed up by killing Dr. Frank Thurber. He held the 32 revolver in his hand, five live rounds still chambered in the cylinder. He pondered taking his own life. The entire incident seemed surreal—he reflected on the event: true enough he had been drinking, yet not drunk; he told himself it seemed like self defense; had Marshall gone for a gun a moment before I shot? The faint, however intense, crowd vitriol convinced him a self defense claim would not stand. He thought of Sara, his brother James, and their plans to gain a better life.

The lanterns were now closing in, from both sides, and the constant yelping of a blood hound told Charley he would soon be discovered. A half-dozen yellow flickering lights lurked just twenty yards away on either side. He decided to stand, arms raised in submission. A commanding voice joined the dog's growl. "Remain perfectly still Charley...got you in my sights."

Charley was pulled from the bushes, hands tied behind his back, and a noose drawn tight around his neck to assure his return to the sheriff. The posse surrounded him as two deputized officers took him to the main street of Aral. The prosecutor read the arrest warrant aloud and asked if Charley had any final requests before he was taken on the Dewar to jail in Frankfort.

"I'd like to have a time to speak with my wife, please."

Charley Wright was somber, penitent and sober as he delivered his request. Sheriff Case enjoyed the moment immensely, apprehending the killer hours after the crime, photographers, and newspaper people recording every detail of the pursuit and capture. He thought...*this could launch me into a big city job!*

Charley Wright was given a half-hour to meet privately with his wife Sara near their home tethered to two armed, watchful officers.

Sara cried uncontrollably for several minutes while hugging her husband. Charley held her and sang a love song quietly in her ear. He finished singing, looked into her eyes and declared, "If you follow my plan exactly as I told you, I *will* return and we will be together once more." He was calm, relaxed and confident as he brushed away the tears streaming down Sara's face.

"Can you really promise me that Charley?" She lifted her head off his chest to see his face.

"Trust me, trust my brother James, and we *will* be together again... I promise."

"Time to go Charley, wrap it up." The sheriff motioned to the deputies to escort Charley to the Dewar and tie him to the aft rail for the ride to Frankfort.

The Dewar pushed off the Aral mill dock and chugged back to Frankfort around 11:30 p.m. A half-moon shone brightly and reflected on the calm water as the ship maneuvered a mile off shore and headed south-south west. Charles T. Wright appeared to be a different man following his arrest. He sat alone, saying very little and humming his favorite songs while he studied the waters off South Manitou Island. There were no signs of the "old" Charley Wright— combative, angry, boisterous, and belligerent. Rather he was reflective, thoughtful, even polite... both Sheriff Case and Prosecutor Covell noted the change.

* * *

I shut down the company store that following Wednesday, when the trial of Charles T. Wright got underway in Benzonia. No one in support of Charley Wright was in the courtroom, except for me. I told my emotional sister to stay home. The lynch-mob mentality prevailed throughout Benzie County. The prosecution moved along confident their case was "air-tight", yet several flaws in their tactics and claims gave Wright's lawyers grounds for appeal. After months of legal maneuvering, the prosecution and defense lawyers made their arguments. Nevertheless, he was convicted on April 30, 1890 of the first degree murder of Dr. Frank Thurber. Wright was sentenced, the next day, to state prison at Jackson, Michigan for the remainder of his natural life.

* * *

Sara kept to herself for almost three weeks after the murders. She was as much embarrassed as afraid. I worried about her and made daily trips to her home to bring food and talk with her. Despite all her disappointment in Charley she continued to pine for him. Something about Charley Wright held a magical bond with my sister. A week after the trial Charley's brother James came over to Aral by steamer from Racine and met with Sara. He was successful in getting her out a little more, frequently walking the shoreline north of town and talking. Twice he drove her in a horse carriage to Traverse City and visited with Charley where he was held awaiting the results of his trial.

The mill ran more or less leaderless for the rest of the summer and fall season. James Wright provided support and some direction, although infrequently, based on his travel schedule. I helped out as a liaison between James and the mill workers for a while. Shortly after the first snow fall in late 1889 the mill was closed for the winter.

CHAPTER--TWELVE

Aral Michigan, May 1, 1890

The two prison officers were an impressive sight; big, muscular men, well armed, square-jawed, and each holding an arm of Charles T. Wright as he was transported to railcar built as a jail dedicated for prisoners in transit. Charley had chain leggings, wrist shackles chained to a neck collar which severely impaired his movement, and a stripped jump suit that had "prisoner" embroidered across his back. As I watched from the train station I felt ill with the message I had to deliver to Charley from my sister. He saw me approach and stood with one guard while the other filled out some paperwork.

"Fred...it's good to see you. How is Sara?" I ignored the question, for the moment.

"You doing Okay Charley?"

"Oh yeah, going on a little trip... downstate to see the beautiful Jackson area, ever been there?" Throughout it all Charley still had a smile, a weird sense of humor, and a positive attitude.

"Charley I have some news from Sara for you."

"Really, great, how is she doing through all this?" His smile retreated a bit.

"Charley, Sara's filing for divorce. I'm sorry to be the one to tell this."

For a brief moment Charley appeared to tear up, yet he held it back, smiled again and said, "Hell Fred, you've been a good friend. I'd rather hear it from you than anyone else I reckon." He looked at me and I could see the first indication that the punishment for his actions was having an emotional impact.

"Tell Sara I love her...and I wish her the best. Oh yeah, tell her I'll see her again one day." The familiar Charley

Wright personality broke through once more with a strong smile, flashing eyes and a confident tone in his voice.

Somewhat startled, yet attentive, I said, "You bet Charley I'll tell her everything you said."

After small, measured steps in chains, Charley climbed the short staircase to the railcar. The iron door slam shut and the guards locked it for the journey to Jackson. He would spend the next ten years in prison at Jackson working as the bookkeeper in the prison's office.

* * *

The ride back to Aral was extra long and painful for me. I replayed my full life experience with Charley Wright. Despite all my misgivings about my sister falling in love and then marrying the rabble-rousing Charley Wright, I missed what I knew he did for her. She was truly happy, even when the "ugly" Charley emerged from drinking, or fighting, or an unwelcome stare. She found the one small part of Charley's personality that was loving, romantic, and caring. I feared she may never recover.

CHAPTER--THIRTEEN

Jackson Michigan Prison, May 1890 through June 1900

Charles and James Wright say their final words before Charley is imprisoned.

* * *

James Wright recovers a large, hidden cache of recovered Westmoreland twenty-dollar gold coins after his brother's arrest and returns to Racine Wisconsin. The Racine lumber mill expands its customer base throughout the Great Lakes.

* * *

Sara Wright divorces Charley Wright out of humiliation. She remarries for security, but not for love, to a local business man in the Aral area.

Charles and James Wright concoct a plan.

CHAPTER—FOURTEEN

Detroit Michigan, Summer 1900

Charles T. Wright became a model prisoner since his incarceration in 1890. His circumstances prohibited the consumption of any alcohol, and together with his middle-aged appearance added to his image as a mature, bright, verbally skilled manager. Things were much clearer for him now. He was able to view his earlier life in perspective, fully recognizing his weakness, abuses and his *strengths*. The prison authorities also saw these qualities and allowed him to supervise certain inmate meetings, gatherings and study sessions. Charles T. Wright was mellowing as a prison inmate.

Most significantly Charley was appointed to the position of prison bookkeeper, which allowed him frequent opportunities to communicate by mail with his brother James.

During the summer of 1900, after years of thought, a plan to secure Charley's release from prison took shape. James made several extended trips to the prison to meet with his brother. It was a bold plan at first inspection, but further reflection suggested the perfect set of circumstances were coming together for a single chance to gain his freedom once more.

First, Charley spent years organizing his thoughts, committing them to paper, then re-writing and embellishing key points for another draft. A massive folder of research, and background material preceded the letter's content. James reviewed the material, commented and suggested changes. The brothers re-worked, refined, and finalized the plan, testing every assumption, anticipating every contingency. The more Charley read it the more he felt his release was at hand. James was committed to pull it off for his brother, and displayed the level-headed, sober thinking needed to accomplish it. Finally the letter was ready. The timetable for action had begun.

James made the meeting appointment with Michigan Governor Hazen S. Pingree for July 8th, a Monday. Pingree had a sterling resume, starting with his service in the Union Army in 1862. He had fought in General Pope's Northern Virginia Campaign, followed by numerous other campaigns until his assignment to the Second Corps, Third Division, in the Army of the Potomac, where he was captured by Confederate forces and spent two years in prisons throughout the south. He later escaped pretending to be someone else during a roll call for a prisoner exchange in November 1864. He rejoined his regiment, fought in more battles, and was present when General Lee surrendered at Appomattox on April 9, 1865. He was an American hero.

* * *

James Wright sat outside the Governor's office waiting to be called in. An attractive, young woman in a full skirt, pulled very tight at the waste, with strawberry hair shaped in long curls flashed a smile. "Mr. Wright?"

"Yes, I'm James Wright." James stood erect and smiled, straightening his three piece suit.

"I'm Deborah, the Governor's administrative assistant. Please follow me to the Governor's office.

The walk was a path through hallways and past conference rooms to a large double set of wooden doors. Deborah knocked politely then opened the doors. Governor Pingree walked from behind his desk and greeted me.

"Hello Mr. Wright. I'm Hazen Pingree. This fellow here is Geoffrey Jones, deputy Attorney General. He has reviewed your letter and I thought he might be able to assist in your request."

Charley and James had anticipated the Governor might seek legal advice before considering a request for a pardon, so James adjusted his early remarks accordingly. Pingree sat down and Jones opened the discussion.

"I understand you are seeking a review of Charles T. Wright's prison sentence, attempting to gain a pardon. He is your brother, is that correct?" Jones was a skinny, tall, angular man with a crooked smile and dark, deep-set eyes. His entire demeanor and appearance said...*don't trust him...*and James took notice.

"Yes he is, and I believe there are compelling reasons to grant a pardon." The direct approach worked exactly as the brothers expected, Jones stiffened, became defensive and cocked his head as he formulated his next remark.

"Well, I see. Have you consulted an attorney on your request or to get a legal opinion?" Jones was now smirking and leaning forward in his chair, mimicking a judge about to throw a case out. James maintained a respectful, disciplined manner; very different than the reactions he felt his brother, the *old* Charley Wright, would have offered.

"No, not really sir, although we do believe our case is compelling."

"And why is that Mr. Wright?" Jones looked annoyed; the governor also noticed the attitude from his deputy AG.

James maintained his cool, calm delivery and prepared his next remark.

James decided to drop the powerful, hidden clues. “The circumstances surrounding the *Aral Mill murders* suggest false eyewitness testimony, which negatively foreshadowed my brother’s argument he was acting in self defense.”

“Hey wait a minute. Charles Wright ran the Aral Mill right? That’s *your* brother?” The governor broke in, as he remembered something, and became very animated.

“Yes, he worked very closely with Matt Pullman and Brad Jackson.” The emotional link was made. The governor’s face flushed as he could not control a smile spreading across his mouth. Jones took no noticed and pawed through papers to form another question.

“Yes, I know the folks involved with that lumber yard. Fine men. Very reliable.” The governor sat back, lit a massive cigar and reflected in silence. James remained still, letting the governor collect his thoughts.

Just as Jones adjusted his wire rimmed glasses before launching another side-tracking question, the governor took control of the discussion.

"Well, I'm not sure I can promise much more than a thorough look at your material Mr. Wright, but if you leave me your letter and material I'll go over it. Fair enough?"

Jones looked confused to see his boss dismiss the meeting so abruptly but appeared delighted he didn't have to personally deny the request out of hand. Pingree stood abruptly and offered his hand.

"Thank you for your time Governor Pingree. Mr. Jones." James knew he delivered the subliminal message and was ready for the next move. Jones stood and walked to the office door with James.

"Goodbye Mr. Wright." Jones gave a brief, firm handshake as he stared over his glasses at James and went on about his day.

Once outside the governor's office, James lingered a moment pretending to organize his briefcase, until the governor's door slowly opened. Pingree peered out and seeing that Jones had left motioned James to return. Deborah smiled and went back to her typing. Pingree quickly ushered James back into his office and retrieved a fresh cigar as James took a chair.

During this session, Pingree sat in front of his desk alongside James Wright. "How is your brother, James? He's in Jackson prison?" The question had a tone of concern.

"He's quite well all things considered." James paused hoping Pingree had more to share.

"You know Matt and Brad are very good friends of mine. We go way back, and I understand the Aral mill actually supplied the lumber for my shoe company's expansion in 1888. That growth spurt, after our fire the year before kept us in front of our competition. Matt and Brad have great respect for your brother." Governor Pingree lowered his eyes reflecting on his good fortune.

The conversation progressed exactly as James and Charles had hoped; a grateful former customer, with strong connections to men who stood up for Charles Wright and his accomplishments. The Pingree and Smith Shoe Company, now owned by Hazen's son, Joe, generated annual sales over $1,000,000. An achievement aided in large part by Charley Wright's promises to deliver massive lumber shipments when needed. By the 1890's, the firm had become the region's largest shoe manufacturer.

Hazen Pingree was beloved by his Michigan voters, and particularity in Detroit, his home town, where he had served as major through four consecutive terms. His business and political followers often said...*Pingree knew how to treat friends.*

"You're aware I plan to not seek re-election this fall?" Pingree was heading in the desired direction. He inhaled a long draw through his cigar and stood to stroll to his office window.

"I believe I did hear that governor. You've done a good job for this state." James withheld a tight grin as the governor glanced over to him. The silence hung in the air for an uncomfortable period.

"I also know about prison life. I spent many years in southern state prisons as a young man...during the war. Prison is hell." The tone of Pingree's voice was sorrowful. "Has your brother been a model prisoner?"

"The best... the very best." James was empathic. Again an uncomfortable silence stalled the conversation.

"Mr. Wright, leave your letter, but take all your backup material and research with you. Mention this meeting to no one except your brother...understood?" Pingree looked forcefully into James' face.

"I do understand sir, thank you for your consideration." James offered his hand; the governor grasped it firmly, and said, "I expect you and your brother may enjoy a New Year's drink."

* * *

On January 1, 1901, his final day in office, Governor Hazen S. Pingree, in his last official act, granted a full and immediate pardon to Charles T. Wright, briefly sighting discrepancies in eye witness accounts during the trial. Charles T. Wright was a free man.

Six months later while in London, England, after returning from an African safari, Hazen S. Pingree died in a London hospital while being treated for peritonitis. He never provided a formal declaration of his decision to pardon Charles T. Wright.

CHAPTER--FIFTEEN

Aral Michigan, March, 1901

The weather had changed. The longer late winter days occasionally produced strong sunlight to melt the snow which arrived almost every other day. I stood ready to sweep the heavy wet snow off the company store porch, even though the town was void of travelers and the mill had not operated at full capacity in seven years. Just as I noticed the warm sun reaching my face I heard an unusual sound.

I hadn't even thought of Charles T. Wright in months, or even years. He was lost to us, as was the mill. Sara had remarried and seemed happy, even though she seldom laughed or smiled as she did when married to Charley. I never expected to see Charley Wright ride into my little town and stop by the company store I continued to operate. Yet, there he was, coming directly toward me. He was driving a new electric coach along with his brother James from Wisconsin. I immediately noticed he was well dressed in expensive clothes, polished leather boots, a top hat and fine soft leather gloves. I stood on the company store porch wielding a shovel to remove the six inches of fresh snow that fell at night. He shut the contraption off, opened the door, got out and walked up to me.

"Hello Fred? It's been quite awhile. Do you remember my brother James?"

He seemed like the *same old* Charley, yet different in a *good* sort of way. I looked at James remembering he'd been in my store many times in prior years.

"Charley, I can't believe it's you. You got out... how?" I stood in awe of the man who had been married to my sister. It was Charley, yet I quickly realized it was a *new* Charley.

"How are you Fred?" Charley smiled and spoke with a smooth, calm delivery.

"I'm good, but the mill is a mess, several unsuccessful owners and a fire...business is way down. What are you doing here?"

"I'm headed back to Wisconsin in a few weeks with James, just thought I'd stop in and see the old town." James walked over to the bridge that served the mill, leaving Charley and me alone for a moment. The silence grew palpable until Charley finally asked, "Is Sara still in the area?"

My throat nearly closed up considering whether a lie would be better for all than the truth. Charley felt my tension. He moved closer and calmly remarked, "It's alright Fred; I just want to say hi."

"Charley, she married a dentist a year after you went to prison. They live about a half-mile out of town towards Empire."

I felt my face flushing...did I say the right thing...would Sara want to see him. "She seems happy Charley, what you two had is over."

"I understand Fred. I'm more controlled than I was in the earlier days...trust me."

The shore side town of Aral never regained the glory and jobs that were there when Charley Wright ran the Aral Mill. The business slipped away, and subsequent owners never had the magic, or powers that Wright had to make things happen. The town was dying and I knew it. Seeing Charley now, calm, free, and refined made me wonder what it would have been like had *this* Charley Wright first come to Aral? I convinced myself he had left the lumbering business behind him and was likely considering new business ventures. After a brief walk about town, Charley and James started their electric coach and headed out of town...in the direction of Empire.

* * *

The house was new, yet small, set back fifty yards from the oak-tree lined road in front. The weather was nice, for March, temperature in the high forties, and a partially sunny sky made it comfortable outside. Charley tapped the brass door knocker and waited. After a few moments, the door opened and it was Sara standing speechless in the shadow. She looked as radiant as when Charley last saw her, some ten years earlier.

"Hello Sara, it's Charley, I've been let out."

"Charley, Charley I can't believe it's you. When did you get out?" Sara was very nervous and fearful of what was happening to her emotions.

"I've been out awhile...a New Year's gift from the Governor."

"Why are you here?" Sara's voice began to tremble and her hands shook.

"I told Fred to tell you... what...I'd see you again one day, right? I came to keep my promise." Sara started to sob and shut the door.

Charley stepped back, took off his top hat and cleared his throat. He then began to sing a favorite love song he'd sung for Sara many times before. His clear, full baritone voice had not changed in ten years, and the words touched Sara's heart. She could feel his former *magic* working in her soul again. He was her true love, and she knew it. The marriage she currently maintained had never approached the passion and depth of emotion she felt every day while married to Charley Wright. The singing reached a crescendo just as Sara lost control of her feelings, falling to her knees and crying out for him to stop. Charley continued and Sara made a difficult decision ...she opened the front door again, rushed into Charley's arms, kissing him passionately.

"I've come back for you. We are meant to be together, and I promised you...we *will* be together again... our day will come...well it has come. I will take care of you till I die."

Sara sobbed for several minutes, held in Charley's arms, frequently kissing him and whispering to him while holding his rugged face in her hands. In a final act of compassion, Sara wrote a long heartfelt note trying to explain to her current husband why she had to leave with Charley; and that she had never really left Charley just that he was jerked out of her life. His reappearance ignited a dormant, yet vital part of her life...a part she could not live without. After thirty minutes, Sara was ready to leave with a small satchel of jewelry and clothes. James watched in a trance-like state as his brother persuasively regained the lost love of his life in less than an hour with little more than a song and a promise. Unbelievable!

* * *

By June, Charley and Sara had settled near the outskirts of Racine, Wisconsin where Charley prospered in dry goods. He never drank again and became a popular vocalist at civic events.

In ten years, the lumbering towns along Lake Michigan's shores were dying, and by 1911, the Aral mill shut down permanently. The last residents left Aral in 1922.

The End

About the Author

Richard Trevae

Trevae presents a suspenseful world of espionage and intrigue, with protagonist Dalton Crusoe and draws on his extensive travels. His journeys have provided a rich backdrop for the exotic locales featured in his novels.

The ARAL MILL MURDERS is based on documented historical events dating from 1854 to 1901, that provide an interesting confluence of events involving a ship wreck, a double murder, and a pardon for the killer—all staged in the lost town of Aral at Otter Creek, within the Sleeping Bear Dunes national lakeshore.

Part adventurer, part businessman, part author, Trevae is an engineer-businessman with an MBA in Finance and Management. Trevae matured a startup design/construction/development firm into a publicly traded company that later merged with a much larger NYSE company. His articles concerning business valuation, mergers, acquisitions, and management practices have been published in various trade associations and business newspapers.

Writing "reality inspired fiction" has become his latest passion. Mr. Trevae lives with his wife along the picturesque shores of Lake Michigan where he is at work on his next book.